Bernhardt Laufer

The White Indian

Bernhardt Laufer

The White Indian

ISBN/EAN: 9783337335021

Printed in Europe, USA, Canada, Australia, Japan

Cover: Foto ©Andreas Hilbeck / pixelio.de

More available books at **www.hansebooks.com**

—THE—

WHITE INDIAN

—^—

WILD WEST DRAMA

—IN—

FOUR ACTS.

BY BERNHARDT LAUFER.

WM. SINNHOLD, Translator.

BUFFALO, N. Y.
1889.

DRAMATIS PERSONÆ.

PROLOGUE.

HENRY ROBERSON, a trapper.
BILL NEWTON, an outcast.
BLOODY TIGER, an Indian chief.
MICHAEL KRAFT, a German laborer.
MINNIE, wife of Roberson.
MARY, sweetheart of Michael.
LITTLE GEORGE, son of Roberson.

SECOND PART.

(*Time, fifteen years later.*)

SHARP EYE, the White Indian.
HENRY REBOR, formerly Roberson.
JOE MORTIMER, formerly Newton.
DUTCH MICHAEL, servant of Roberson.
FLYING DEER, an Indian.
RALPH,
JIM, } Mortimer's companions.
SAM WILSON, a sheriff.
PAT, a bartender.
ALICE, Roberson's niece.
MARY, wife of Michael.
Trappers, Sheriffs, Indians, Bandits, Tramps, Etc.

ACT I.

SCENE I. *A room in a block house. Door and window in rear.*

MINNIE *seen sitting at a table, her child playing at her feet.*

Minnie. Oh, will this terrible suspense never close? My God, what does it mean? Henry has been absent for more than a week, and this anxiety if not soon terminated, will surely drive me mad. What can detain him so long? My anxiety is hourly increasing. Can the Indians have molested or captured him; oh what a dreadful thought! His fearlessness and great love for hunting often prompt him to wander far from home, beyond the lines to the camps of the Indians. Then the news that Captain Newton, the terror of the prairie, the evil doer and outlaw, is preying around here again, further increases my alarm. He is a tiger in human form, and human blood is ravishing lust to his instincts. Would to God that the white men and Indians in this vicinity would unite and annihilate that beastly monster.

George. Oh, mamma; if I ever meet that bad man, I'll tell him what I think of him.

Minnie. What a thought, my precious child!

5

George. Papa and Uncle William often spoke about that bad man, mamma, and papa said he was awful wicked and should be killed. If I was a big man, mamma, I wouldn't let him frighten you. I'd hunt him down and shoot him with papa's rifle.

Minnie. There, there, love, you mustn't speak so. The bad man want harm us. (*aside*) What portentous words! the child talks so strange; what can it mean? His childish prattle seems to contain a prophecy. May heaven interfere and save us from harm!

Bloody Tiger. (*appears in the door.*)

Minnie. [*aside.*] An Indian? Who is he and what does his presence signify; does he bring tidings of Henry?

Bloody Tiger. Ugh! hello, white woman, Indian tired and hungry. Can he get something to eat, and a place to rest?

Minnie. [*aside.*] He would speak in a different tone if he knew aught of poor Henry. (*to Indian.*) I am sorry, I cannot supply your wants.

Bloody Tiger. Oh, white woman, have pity on a poor Indian who is starving.

Minnie. No, no, I dare not shelter you, or offer you succor. My husband despises and hates your race, and should he return and find you here, he would treat you like a dog. He would be offended if I should extend any hospitality to a red man.

Bloody Tiger. Oh, white woman, do not drive me away hungry and weary. Just a little food and a few hours rest for a poor Indian. Your husband is a long journey from here, –down the river–and will not return while I am here.

George. Ma, let him rest here and give him something to eat; he must be very hungry and tired, and papa will not drive him out if he returns to find him here.

Minnie. Well, well; as ever the child pleads for you. I will keep you, but if my husband returns and finds you here, I won't be responsible for what may happen. Sit down and eat all you want. (*Bloody Tiger eats.*)

[*enter Roberson.*

Roberson. Hello, red skin! what are you doing here? (*after embracing his wife and child, continues.* Did you find what you were hunting for, red skin, or do you want me to help you find something that you never lost?

Bloody Tiger. A poor Indian found what he was looking for—shelter and food.

7

Roberson. Indeed! come, tell us, what is your name and to what tribe does my brave red brother belong?

Bloody Tiger. My name is Eagle-head. I am a warrior of the great Apache nation!

Roberson. You lie! do you want me to tell you who you are? Oh, I know you, Bloody Tiger, chief of the Cherokees! Your tribe is on the war-path, and now tell me what your mission is!—What! you want speak? then begone from here, or I'll show you how a white man can protect his home and family. (*turning aside momentarily, Roberson puts himself in peril, as the Indian chief endeavors by stealth to stab him. Georgie realizes the situation, grasps his father's rifle and levels it at the warrior.*)

George. Down with your knife or I'll shoot! (*Roberson draws a revolver and faces the savage. The latter hastily retreats.*)

Roberson. That's right, my boy! Keep him ten feet away from you.

Bloody Tiger. You'll suffer for this, all of you; and soon, too. [*exit.*

Minnie. A dangerous fellow, that,—we must guard against him, for he means mischief.

Roberson. Dangerous indeed, and this will serve as a good lesson for you. Henceforth,

8

keep such varmints from the door.

George. Pa, may I see which way he went? I am not afraid of him.

Roberson. Well, my little man, go then, but do not venture out of sight of the house. (*exit George*) Happy, innocent child! I greatly fear that the time will come when he, too, will tremble with fear and his breast will be heavy. My dear wife, did you hear the latest news about Capt. Newton?

Minnie. No, Henry, I did not; my thoughts were entirely about your safety. I heard that he was again prowling around here, and I became very much alarmed. But I can see by your looks, that something has happened. What is it?

Roberson. Well, calm your fears, for he will never harm anybody. He is dead.

Minnie. Dead, you say, can it be true? oh, what a blessing to all of us. His very name inspired fear and hate.

Roberson. Well, it is only too true, for brother William and I sent him to hell to keep company with many of his bad companions. He will never more trouble us.

Minnie. Is it possible? Was that the cause of your long absence?

9

Roberson. Yes, my dear, and if you care to hear it, I'll tell you the whole story. When 1 left you about a week ago, in order to go hunting; I met William, who told me that he was on Newton's trail. I agreed to join him. We had a long chase after him, but we finally located him and his companions. We attacked them, and after a desperate fight, Capt. Newton was captured and one of his companions killed. We decided to take our prisoner to the fort, but on the way thither, he managed to elude our vigilance and attempted to escape. We overtook him on the bank of the river. Being in eminent danger of re-capture, he plunged into the river and vainly endeavored to swim to the opposite bank. To aim and fire at him was the act of a few seconds; and with a frantic scream, he sank under the water, never to rise again. Our bullets sped true, for we watched the surface of the river in all directions, for some time; but to no purpose. Fully satisfied of his death, we started homeward.

Minnie. Husband, how happy I am that no harm came to you and that, that dangerous man is silenced forever. Henry, tell me; did you not fear to meet that rascal when out hunting alone?

Roberson. Why, what a little coward you are! No, Minnie, why should I fear to meet him? To be sure, I always tried to avoid him and always kept on my guard. He was an ugly chap to deal with, and the community will hail his death with gratification. And now, my dear, I have to leave you for a little while; as I must hasten to the fort, to announce Newton's death. While I am there, I'll try to get a man-servant who will protect you and Georgie when I am away from home. So, good-bye, dearest for a brief period.

Minnie. Oh, Henry; must you leave us so soon? Please stay till to-morrow at least. My mind is sorely troubled, and I have terrible forebodings and a presentiment of some dire affliction. Do not go; I entreat you!

Roberson. Do'nt agitate yourself unnecessarily, for there is nothing to fear. Those red devils and wandering spirits have fled. Fear not, and I'll soon return.

Minnie. Well, husband dear, if I cannot persuade you to stay, I'll accompany you a little way—as far as the clearing.

[*exeunt Minnie and Roberson.*

Newton. [*appearing suddenly, peers around, and seeing nobody, soliloquizes:*]

11

Nobody about the place? I would like to know if the villan returned here, after his murderous attack on me. Stupid fool to think that I am dead and gone; Ha, ha, ha! I am not so easily drowned, and the lead that is to finish me, has not yet been mined. But I will wreak vengeance on him and his; yes, bloody revenge will I seek. Food for the hungry buzzards, they will make. I am sorry for my poor companion's fate. Those damned cowards led us a fearful chase. They hunted us like a couple of wild beasts. I had a close call for my life and I swallowed enough water to float myself, I guess. But I wasn't born to be drowned. Here I am and I shall effect a bloody settlement with all of my pursuers. I am not thirsty; but I'll dye the soil with their crimson life blood, or my name is not Bill Newton. (*footsteps heard, and Minnie re-appears.*) She must be that fellow's wife. I'll speak to her. (*louder.*) Well, ma'am, has your husband returned? I met him in the woods, about two hours ago.

Minnie. Yes sir, he did come home; but he went to the fort to report Capt. Newton's death.

Newton. Ha, ha, he did! eh? He's gone on a fool's errand; but I guess you will do,—so get on your duds and come with me.

Minnie. Sir, what do you mean! Speak open-
ly like a man, or I may may think you are a
boy!

Newton. You have a sharp tongue, my dear
lady, and you know very well how to use it.
I'll tell you what I mean. I mean to take
you away from your home and all them you
love. (*lifts his hands to take hold of her. Minnie makes a quick step and pulls a revolver out of
his belt.*)

Minnie. Take care! Now,—you go!

Newton. Yes, I will,—but only with you. [*they
wrestle,—he secures the pistol and runs after her.*

George. [*appearing at window.*] Mamma, mamma, pa is coming, and a lot of soldiers from
the fort, are with him. They are coming fast,
too. Come and see. Hello! Hurrah!

Newton. The devil! If that is the case, I must
not be seen here, and I'll stand upon the
order of my going; but go at once. [*exit.*

Minnie. Dear Georgie, is it really so? Is your
father coming back? Where is he?

George. [*smiling.*] No, mamma, that was a ruse
of mine. I saw that bad man chasing and
frightening you, and I only said it to scare

13

him away.   Wasn't it funny to see him go so quick?

Minnie.   Dear, dear little fellow!   You are just like your father, and will be as brave as a lion! You have saved the lives of your parents this day, and may God bless you for it.   What a blessing it is to have good children!

SCENE II.   *An opening in the forest.*

MARY *and* MICHAEL *enter.*

[*Both speak broken.*]

Mary.   [*entering from the right.*]   Hello Dutchman!

Michael.   [*unseen.*]   Hello Dutch girl! (*enter Michael from the left, rushes up and kisses her.*)

Mary [*angerly.*]   Leave me alone you nasty fellow; I dont want to here your voice again, I dont want to see you and you shant kiss me either.

Michael.   [*smiling.*]   Nah, Nah! Mary, what's the matter with you,—what coon has taken possession of joy?

Mary.   No coon like you!   I don't want you to annoy me again; I am no Dutch girl!

Michael.   Is that so!   Well, what are you,—a boy?

14

Mary. No, I am a German girl; do you understand?

Michael. Well, what of it? What am I? Who called me Dutch first? Oh, well, I understand now. You've read about the Flying Dutchman, and when you saw me, it came back to you.

Mary. Not at all; that would be flattery, but as soon as I saw you I could not help thinking of the Dutch Michael!

Michael. That's better yet; you called me Den Deutschen Michael, well that is more than I can claim, for he was a brilliant soldier; while I am only a second hand back-woods laborer.

Mary. [*offended.*] I say; your name is Michael Fool!

Michael. So it is, and coumpany, but hark girl; what brought you here anyhow?

Mary. My two little feet if you must know!

Michael. Little feet? Ha, ha, that is the biggest joke of the season!

Mary. Well, if you will stop laughing I'll tell you my business here. I came to meet you, this is your birthday, Michael, and I thought it no more than right to show you my devotion and love, by giving you a little present.

15

(*opens her basket and hands him a little box wrapped in colored paper.*)

Michael. My beloved Mary! My heart leaps like a jumping-jack, I thank you so much, you are the only one in this wide world who thinks of Michael. But my love, why did you not speak of the present at first, only think we lost at least fifteen precious minutes of hugging and kissing. [*trys to kiss her.*

Mary. Stop! Ungrateful wretch, you mus'nt kiss me; and you sha't open that box in my presence. I must go now. I'll see you again to-night, and then I'll listen to your squeals, good-bye Michael. Good-bye!

Michael. By, by! Don't be in such a hurry! Bless me, if she is'nt out of sight already. She is a sweet, good girl. I'll bet there is something nice in this box, for she has exquisite taste. Well, lets see what is in here.

(*Henry appears, and stops him from opening the box.*)

Roberson. Say, young fellow; don't you know a good man around here, who would like to get work?

Michael Oh yes! Take me, I am just looking for a place. I tell you I can swing an ax as good as all the other boys, and I am afraid of nothing!

16

Roberson.   Well, that is just the man I want to get; but say, are you strong and healthy?

Michael.   Why sure, my name is Michael Kraft and "Kraft" means strength   If I am heathy you can find out easy, when you go down and ask my "landsman" what I can eat in a day.

Roberson.   Ha, ha, ha! You are a jolly fellow and I like your style; but how is it,—can you handle a gun?

Michael.   Handle a gun?   Why, mein Gott, that is nothing for me.   You must understand that I was a soldier ten month's old when I left Germany.

Roberson.   Oh, I see; you are one of those runaways too, eh?

Michael.   Yes, I don't deny it!   I made room, you know, for another one.

Roberson.   I must say you have a very kind heart,—if this is the cause of your coming to this country.

Michael.   Yes, yes, that is so; my little girl found it out too.

Roberson.   What! you have a girl, a child?

Michael.   No, I mean my sweet heart; and you bet she is my darting!   I am going to make

17

her my wife, as soon as I get a shop. When
you take me, everything is all right between
me and Mary.

Roberson. I would like to hire you, but I don't
know if you are willing to work for me.

Michael. Well, if I work for you or for somebody else, that is all the same. I have got to
work anywhere; no matter where I go to.

Roberson. That is the talk of a straight fellow!
The work you have to do is not very hard;
for you only have to protect my family when
I am out hunting. Now, I want you to go
there in a short time. The place, you will
find about fifteen miles from here, and it is
known as Roberson's ranch. [*exit.*

Michael. Allright! allright, Mister! I can keep
that in my head well enough. That is what
I call luck, it is the first luck I got in this
country! I hope it will not run away from
me like Mary did before. Oh, I very near forgot her present! (*opens the box, disclosing a
black jumping jack.*) Well, now, that is a deifel of a present! You are handsomer than the
Flying Dutchman and Dutch Michael. (*shuts
the box and tossing it to a lady in the audience.*)
Please keep it, for Michael's sake! [*exit.*

Scene III.   *A forrest sbene.   Exterior view of the block house.*

Bloody Tiger [*sneaking around the house, disappears, and reappears with Newton.*] The woman and child are in the house, but the white hunter is still absent.

Newton.   Iknow better, only a little while ago ˙ I heard the boy halloing to his mother, that his father was coming with soldiers.

Bloody Tiger.   Ugh, little devil has a crooked tougne, he was playiug a trick on you, in order to get you away from his mother and out of the house.

Newton.   Beware, redskin, dont tell any yarns! How can you account for that!

Bloody Tiger.   Because I watched the house from a distance, from the time I left it.   All three were out at one time and the womnn returned alone; now she and her boy are in there.

Newton.   Well, redskin, I want you to go in and put an end to both of them.   I'll remain outside and warn you in time, should any one approach.

Bloody Tiger   Do the deed yourself! I shall not do such murderous work.

19

Newton. What, you refuse? you want do it? Oh, well, I forgot—here take this and when you are through with the job, I'll give you more of that glittering stuff. (*offers gold.*)

Bloody Tiger. (*indignantly throws the gold at Newton's feet.*) Thunder and lightning! Red men are not as bad as white men. The red man is not a slave for money like the white man. (*Newton attempts to draw revolver.*) Keep your hands off (*revolver in hand.*) I am no robber, and I will not rob any person of life, to please another; but I will have revenge. I will steal the child and bring him up as an Indian, who shall hate and fight against his own brothers. (*to Newton.*) You may settle with his parents in any manner you please, for all I care.

Newton. Hurry up, Tiger, kill them quick, and I'll give you a fortune.

Bloody Tiger. Stop your talk, a brave Indian is not a villian! you can buy plenty of white men for such base work, but an Indian, never. You are coward!

Newton. What, you dare call me a coward? I'll show you that I have even more courage than a redskin! (*can't find his knife.*) Let me take your knife for only five minutes, I lost mine.

Bloody Tiger. Lost your knife? that's good, but here take this. (*hands knife to Newton, and approaches the house. Georgie comes out and is grasped by Newton, who hands him to the Indian.*)

George. Ma, oh ma, come help Georgie!

Minnie. [*rushing forth from the house.*] Georgie, oh Georgie, where are you?

Newton. [*springing towards her.*] Here, woman stop your noise and come with us!

Minnie. Ha! you are the same stranger who was here before. Villain! what did you do with my boy?

Newton. Your boy is in my power, and you too are my captive.

Minnie. Wretch, how dare you say so; I'm in your power? Never!

Newton. Ha, ha, my beauty, my name is Captain Newton, and I will not be foiled; now my sweet damsel come with me,—my chance for revenge has improved. (*Newton endeavors to slay her with the knife. She struggles with him and manages to secure the knife.*) Here you jade, give me back that knife! [*draws pistol.*

Minnie. Stop you villain! Do not be alarmed, I will not escape; I know it would not save me from death! Die, I must, I can read this in your face; and therefore I'd rather die by

21

my own hands, than by the hands of a coward who has the courage to lift them against a powerless woman!

Newton. By jiminy, she is keeping her word; she is killing herself. (*Minnie thrusts the knife into her bosom and falls to the ground.*) What a pity to be deprived of the fun of doing that job. She is a slick one, and has done the work very neatly; there is a pleasure in lessening the number of my fellow creatures, for by doing so I decrease the number of my foes, but as it is, I am just as well satisfied, for my hands are not stained from her blood!

Bloody Tiger. Come away, quick! I hear footsteps in the distance, coming this way.

[*exeunt rapidly.*

Roberson. [*entering hurriedly.*] I thought I heard some one scream. I hope no harm has come to my darling wife and child. (*sees body of his wife.*) By the Almighty, how is this, my wife dead? Murdered! and I came too late to prevent it! Great God, lead me to find the wicked murderer! Oh, lead me to discover the monster, who has thus ruined my home, and blasted the happiness of my life. Oh, that I may soon find him!

22

Newton [*stealing up from behind, plunges knife into Roberson's back.*] You want have to wait long. Here he is, take that! Ha, ha, ha!

Roberson Oh, my God, I have been stabbed! Who, who, stabbed me?

Newton. If any one asks you, tell them that it was I who cut your wife and cut you.

Roberson. [*sees child in the grasp of the Indian.*] Oh, my God, spare my precious child!

George. Pa, dear pa, come help; shoot the man!

Roberson. My poor child, I am powerless to help you. Oh, God give me strength to recognize those devilish butchers; give me strength to punish them. Ha! all is over with me—I am growing faint,—I cannot see, —farewell my child, my— (*he becomes motionless.*) [*exeunt others.*

[*enter Michael singing.*]

Michael. [*unseen.*]

"When all the world is apple pie,"
"And all the sea was ink,"
"When all the trees were bread and cheese"
"What should we have to drink."

Oh, ya, (*yawns*) that's the way the money goes! Here I have been in this country nearly three years, and I cant say I own a nickel; much less a well stocked ranch. (*looking round.*) This must be the house I was looking for; the owner hired me to work for him and to protect the house and family, when he is away. I like the looks of that man, and as he said the work was light, with plenty of pie and cheese to eat, and enough to drink. I hope there are no Paddies around here, I never dread work, but I can't work when Paddies are around; its funny but a Dutchman and an Irishman invariably agree to disagree.

Roberson. [*faintly.*] Help, oh help!

Michael. Mein Gott what was that? Didn't some one call for help? Was there a fight? A nice place to begin work; I don't tihnk I'll stay here, for although I am no coward, I have got a permit to live, and I don't want to surrender it just yet. (*starts to leave, but sees Roberson.*) Mercy, a man lying on the ground! I must find out if it is the man who hired me. By God, yes, it's him! (*bends over him.*) He is covered with blood too, and he seems to be dead! I wonder if it was murder? (*kneels and examines Roberson.*) He still breathes, but very faintly. Poor fellow, wait and I'll help you. (*sees Minnie*) Hello, here is a woman, but she is dead?

Roberson. Help! Give me water. Oh help!

Michael Yes, yes, you shall have water, right
away, double quick! (*stumbles over knife and
picks it up.*] Pampen and Granaten, what's
that? A knife! what a queer looking thing;
but hold, it may be a Godsend, for by means
of this knife, I may be able to reveal this
mystery. I shall not rest till I discover the
secret of this crime. And here in the still-
ness of these woods, I swear that I shall not
give up the pursuit till I bring to justice the
cowardly perpetrator of this devilish deed!

CURTAIN.

ACT II.

A garden scene. Exterior view of a mansion.

[*Enter* HENRY REBOR, ALICE *and* MICHAEL.]

Henry. Welcome, thrice welcome, my darling.
Why, what is the matter with your foot, you
are lame?

Michael. Miss Alice sprained her foot in alight-
ing from her horse.

Alice. It it is only a trifle, there is no danger,
it will soon be all right again.

Henry. What caused you to jump from the
horse? he is very docile; was he frightened?

Alice. I cannot account for it, he suddenly

25

shied and dashed with furious speed across the plain. Then of a sudden he stopped short, reared and I became greatly alarmed. I became faint and I was gently lifted out of the saddle by some strong arm, and on touching the ground I injured my foot. [*Sharp-Eye appears in the back-ground listening.*

Henry. Perhaps it was our neighbor Mr. Mortimer, who hastened to your rescue.

Alice. Dear uncle, please do not mention his name; he is too selfish to do good to anybody. No, uncle, I was assisted by a handsome young man. He is an Indian and he told me that his name was Sharp-Eye. Oh, uncle, is'nt that a romantic name? and such lovely eyes! They are full of pride, fearlessness and honesty. I know that he is worthy of any good woman's love. I do believe that I shall love him. Why, dear uncle what is the matter? you are very much agitated.

Henry. Come to me my darling, sit by my side and I will tell you the cause of my emotion. I long expected that the time would come when I would be compelled to tell you all. It is a long and painful story, but I shall be as brief as possible. A little over fifteen years ago, I was one of the happiest of men; I had a lovely and devoted wife and a bright and handsome boy, who were the light of my home, and the joy of my life. My occupation, that of a trapper, required me to be away from home frequently. On one of these occasions on returning from a brief journey, I was horrified to find my beloved wife lying outside of the cottage, murdered! The ground was dyed crimson with her life blood, which still trickled from a gaping wound in her bosom. I knelt beside her, when the same cowardly assassin stabbed me in the back. After a few blank moments of agony and despair, I summoned strength enough to turn in the direction in which my assailant was fleeing. He had my darling boy in his arms, and as he turned to look back, I recognized the devilish, grinning face of the murderer. He was Sharp-Eye's father!

Alice. Oh uncle, stop, please stop! What a terrible story, I cannot bear to listen to it any longer.

Henry. You must, Alice, you must, for it deeply concerns your future welfare. In all probability, my would be murderer thought I was dying when he saw me sink to the ground. My child, I would have died, had it not been for Michael there who restored me, and to

27

whom I am indebted for my life.

Michael. Do not speak of that again Mr. Rebor, for the slight service I rendered you has been repaid a thousand times.

Henry. As soon as I was able to get on my feet again we started for your parents' home. On arriving there, we found them dead, having been murdered by Sharp-Eye's father, Bloody Tiger!

Alice. Uncle!

Henry. My darling, I am speaking the truth. I searched for him a whole year, and at last I found him. My first inquiry was after my son. His reply was, 'Look for him under the ground.' I overcome with fury; I killed him with this, his own knife, (*shows Alice the knife, lays it on the bench.*) which he left after committing his murderous attack on me.

Sharp-Eye. [*aside, makes a motion toward Rebor.* Then it was he who killed my father! I will kill him! No, no, I cannot do it, I cannot! [*hides himself near the gate.*]

Henry. I searched and researched the whole region in quest of my son, but alas! in vain. God, alone knows, whether he is yet alive. Sharp-Eye is said to be quite intelligent, more so than his father was.

28

Alice. Oh uncle, that is a dreadful story; what a pity that poor Sharp-Eye should be the son of the murderers of my parents.

Michael. Ah, I see Mr. Mortimer, our neighbor, coming this way.

Alice. Please, uncle allow me to go into the house, I dislike that man very much.

Michael. [*aside.*] So do I, I don't like his looks.

Henry. Stay my dear, don't show our neighbor any discourtesy.

Mortimer. [*enters through the gate, and saluting all.*] I am going to leave here for a couple of weeks, and I come to bid you good bye.

Michael. [*aside.*] Oh Lord, only a couple of weeks, why did'nt he say forever?

Mortimer. But before leaving here, Mr. Rebor, I have something to tell you, and I would like to have a little private conversation with you. (*both stepping aside.*) Mr. Rebor, I think that you have divined my feelings towards your lovely niece, Miss Alice. To be sure I am not a young man, but I am rich and independent, and can make her life a luxurious and happy one. Will you permit me to claim her hand and consider her my betrothed?

Henry Your wealth is no inducement as that is offset by our own, and in regard to Miss

29

Alice's affections, if you can win them I shall interpose no objection. Speak to her yourself!

Michael. [*aside.*] I wonder what he is speaking about. Should he demand anything unusual, I tell him something what will make him jump like a horse.

Mortimer. [*approaching Alice.*] Miss Alice, your uncle and I had a little conversation in regard to yourself. [*Michael listening.*

Alice. Indeed, I presume I ought to feel highly flattered. Pray, what was the subject of your interesting conversation.

Mortimer. Dear Alice, you were the subject! I asked your uncle for permission to seek your hand in marriage. Will you make me the happiest of mortals, by becoming my wife?

Alice. Sir, you must not speak thus! I can never be your wife, and you must give up all such ideas.

Mortimer. Do you wish me to understand that I must abandon all hope, that you can never love me?

Alice. Yes sir, I can never bestow my love on a person unworthy of it.

Mortimer. [*perceiving knife on bench, to Michael*] Ah!—say, whose knife is that?

Michael. It belonged to an Indian, who murdered my mistress, and sought to kill my master too.

Mortimer. [*to Henry.*] Then it was you who escaped from death.

Henry. The same, sir!

Mortimer. [*aside.*] Then he must be Roberson whom I thought dead. (*aloud.*) I shall have to leave you now, and for the last time before I go on my journey, I ask you Miss Alice will you become my wife?

Michael. No sir, she would never wed a horse thief!

Mortimer. You damned Dutchman, what do you mean by that?

Michael. Listen and I will tell you. Not long ago I tried to catch a horse thief; I pursued him closely. We met, exchanged some shots, and one of my bullets took effect in the fellows left hand. (*seizing Mortimer's left hand.*) There is the mark! Do you know now what I mean, you Spitz bub!

Mortimer. [*retreating.*] That fellow speaks the truth, I am a thief and robber; you would not give up your niece to me, but I swear she shall yet be mine. (*to Michael.*) I'll settle with you fellow, at my own convenience.

31

Michael. Get off from the premises as quick as you can, or I will make you run as if the deifel was riding on your back.

Mortimer. [*drawing revolver.*] Beware! do not come too close to this toy; I will kill you!

Sharp-Eye. [*emerging and wresting the revolver from Mortimer.*] Go! you have lingered here long enough; your game is up!

Newton. Yes, I see; but that will not keep me back to call some other time!

Sharp-Eye. White man speaks like a fool, he better takes care for himself! Red man is no friend of horse thiefs! [*Sharp-Eye with revolver in hand.*]

Newton. Pshaw! [*exit.*

Alice. Oh, uncle, this is Sharp-Eye who rescued me.

Michael. Thanks to you my brave fellow. You appeared just in the nick of time. Should you ever need my aid, just call upon Dutch Michael!

Henry. I, too owe you thanks, young man, here is my hand.

Sharp-Eye. No sir, I cannot touch your hand, for you know I am the son of Bloody-Tiger!

I must go now, to look after Mortimer. Good bye to all! [*exit.*

Henry. It is strange, very strange, that young man has the skin of an Indian, and the manners of a white man. Come Alice, let us go into the house. [*they go in.*

Michael. She loves the Indian, and I cannot blame her. I myself begin to like the fellow. I would like to do him a good turn. I wonder if he loves Alice. I have it, I got it, I know it, yes; sure I——

Mary. [*at the door.*] Michael where are you? M-i-c-h-a-e-l!

Michael. Hold your tongue, I am busy without you!

Mary. Why Michael, what is the matter?

Michael. Leave me alone!

Mary. Don't be cross, I have something nice for you.

Michael. Come, come, don't bother me. I'm talking business to myself!

Mary. Michael, come quick, your best meal is waiting for you.

Michael. What? Sauerkraut and Speck! why did you not say so right away, and not leave

33

me so long in suspense? I'll come, yes I'll come darling. [*laughing and dancing.*

Alice. [*enters and taking a seat.*] Oh, what a dreadful misfortune! To think that Sharp-Eye's father was the murderer of my parents! Yet I cannot help loving him and my heart beats for no one else. I loved him from the very moment I first saw him, and I cannot help thinking of it.

Sharp-Eye. [*appearing and looking about.*] Sweet Prairie Rose!

Alice. You here, Sharp-Eye!

Sharp-Eye. Yes, to warn you and to protect all of you, if possible. The robber, Joe Mortimer will soon be here with some of his gang to make an assault upon the house.

Alice. Oh, I must report this to my uncle at once!

Sharp-Eye. [*intercepting her.*] You must not! You and your uncle must manage to leave the house as soon as possible. Flying-Deer and myself will defend it from within.

Alice. I shall never consent to that, for I am afraid you will get hurt and fall into the power of that wicked Mortimer.

Sharp-Eye. Perhaps you are right, but what of it; who cares for the poor Indian? I want

34

to see all those whom I love, safe and out of danger. I have no doubt but the attack will fail, but you must trust me, and do as I tell you.

Alice. I shall be guided by you, yet I shall remain near by with my uncle and friends. Be very careful will you, and do not expose yourself unnecessarily, for my sake! [*exit.*

[*it is getting dark.*]

Flying Deer. [*entering.*] They are on the way here and you must make haste if you want to stop those fellows from killing your friends.

Sharp-Eye. Well, I am ready! Come, let us prepare to receive them and show them, that we are not so bad as some of the pale-faces. [*both enter the house.*

Mortimer. [*appearing with two companions.*] Everything is in our favor. You, Ralph, conceal yourself, and when opportunity affords, make the best use of your gun and knife.

Ralph. All right, Captain! in case you need my help, whistle and I'll be on hand. [*exit.*

Mortimer. [*to Jim.*] You go around the house and see whether there is anything in our way. Hasten! (*soliloquizing.*) Well, Henry Roberson, for many years, you have believed that Bloody Tiger killed your wife, and you

35

also rested under the false impression that I had been drowned by that plunge in the river. Ha, ha, ha! Well, I did not think that you yet remained among the living. I thought that fifteen years ago I sent you to the grave, but this very night you shall die!

Jim. [*returning.*] All is quiet Captain!

Mortimer. Come then and let no one escape, a few well directed thrusts and our work will be done. But, hark! Should the girl cross your path, do not harm a hair of her head, but bring her to me instantly. [*They seek to enter the house, but suddenly the door opens the two Indians appear with torches and revolvers.*

Sharp-Eye. Stand back! Begone from here, you see we are on guard, and cannot be surprised or overpowered!

Michael. [*appearing with leveled gun.*] Stop a moment, I want to speak to you first!

[*Alice and Henry appear in the back ground; Mary too with a big broom.*

Mary. Michael, look out! he shoots!

[*Ralph emerges and fires aimlessly at Michael without hitting him. Sharp-Eye fires at Ralph, the others hastily retreat.*

36

Henry. [*to Sharp-Eye.*] Our thanks are due to you a second time.

Sharp-Eye. I do not care for your thanks! you well know that I am the son of the man who fell by your own hand.

Henry. Your father killed my wife and others who were dear to me; and not content with that, he also stole my beloved little son, my only child!

Sharp-Eye. And if he did, could you never forgive? You are a white man and the principles of your religion teach you to forgive and not to seek revenge! I, however, am an uncouth, uneducated, and untaught Indian. However, I forgive and pardon you, for all you have done against my father, and here, standing in the presence of the Great Spirit, I declare that I will protect you and your friends against your enemies, even at the sacrifice of my own life!

CURTAIN.

ACT III.

SCENE I. *Interior of a roughly built house.*

JOE *and* JIM *playing cards at a table.*

Ralph. [*entering quickly.*] B-r-r-r b-r-r-r. (*storms*

outside.) Captain, I have to report something that will please you better than anything you have heard for the last two months.

Mortimer. Speak out Ralph, what is it?

Ralph. I saw Dutch Michael in company with his master and niece, looking for shelter from the storm. I think they are coming this way.

Mortimer. What! do you speak the truth?

Ralph. Look there, convince yourself!

Mortimer. [*going to the door.*] The deuce, that is lucky! Yes, they are coming straight towards the house. Once more in my power, no stratagem will save them. Ralph, you manage the girl, and you Jim, take care of the Dutchman; I'll dispose of the old man.

[*Roberson, Michael and Alice enter, are seized and bound.*]

Mortimer. Ah, my old neighbors, you are cordially welcome; but pray what is the object of this most unexpected but doubly welcome visit? (*changing his manner.*) So, at last you have fallen into my power and nothing can save you this time. Time became really tedious without you, but now I am fully repaid. Ha, ha, ha!

Henry. Sir, what have I ever done to you to merit such treatment?

Mortimer. What have you done? What have you not done? Enough sir, to turn me into a monster!

Henry. I never harmed anybody, and you are the first who dares to say otherwise. For God's sake, man, what do you intend to do?

Mortimer. Did you not kill Bloody Tiger, because you took him for the murderer of your wife? but I tell you now you killed the wrong man! It was I who caused your wife to kill herself, and it was I who stabbed you in the back, intending to kill you.

Henry. It is impossible!

Michael. Don't mind what he says, he only wants to vex you. I'm on to him!

Alice. Thank heaven, Sharp-Eye's father did not murder my parents!

Mortimer. It is possible! Do you remember Bill Newton?

Henry. Certainly I do.

Mortimer. I am glad to hear it! I am Bill Newton; once the terror of the prairie, and still alive, and planning mischief.

Henry [*springing towards Newton.*] You villain, now I see why you were terror stricken when you perceived the knife on the bench!

39

Newton. That is true enough, for when I saw that knife, I knew who you were. Now comrades, fasten that fellow to a chair, also take the girl and the Dutchman away from here and meet me at the old rendezvous.

Alice. Oh, my God, what next! Uncle, dear uncle, what are they going to do? Best and dearest of friends, shall I ever see you again?

Henry. Cheer up, my brave girl! Try to keep up your strength and spirits. Have faith and let sorrow not weaken you. God will surely assist us.

Michael. Yes sir; unser Gott will help us, I know it!

Newton. That's enough, take her away!

Alice. [*to Newton.*] Oh, have mercy on us!

Newton. Mercy! There is no such word in my dictionary! [*laughing.*

Michael. Good bye, dear master, we have been of assistance to each other many times in the past, but, alas! in this trying moment I am powerless to aid you. I shall try however to keep my eyes on Miss Alice and guard her against injury.

Newton Stop your lamenting! Boys, take 'em away! [*exeunt Alice and Jim.*

40

Michael. [*to Ralph.*] Nah, nah, don't handle me so rough! I am no beer keg!

Ralph. [*mad.*] Oh, go on, go on! [*exeunt Michael and Ralph.*

Newton. [*to Henry.*] Well sir, we are alone now and I hope for the last time. Pardon me, but I must shut your mouth. (*tying cloth over his mouth.*

Henry. Coward! devil! Curse upon you!

Newton. You are the one who caused me to become a devil! (*places powder keg and fuse.*) Do you notice how skillfully I seek to revenge myself; you must perish with this hut? You and your would-be rescurer will be blown to atoms. By my little arrangement, when the door is opened, you and your rescurer will be shot, and the house blown up. (*screws two blocks with pistols on the floor.*) Say, what do you think of my plan to dispose of you? Your lovely niece will become my mistress as soon you perish. (*ignites the fuse.*) Henry Roberson, a happy journey to you through the invisible regions of the air. [*laughing sardonically, opens the window, leaps out and bars the window. Roberson tries to upset the chair and succeeds. Sharp-Eye appears at the door, calling Batters down the door.   Two shots are heard, but nobody hurt.   Sharp-Eye enters hastily.*

Sharp-Eye.   Ugh! the smell of something burning caused me to force an entrance to this place and here I am nealy shot! (*sees captive in chair and believing he had fired the shots, draws his knife to kill him.   Stops on seeing his helpless condition.*)   No, it was'nt him who fired at me!   Ugh! those blocks and pistols—I understand.   Why, this is the uncle of Alice! (*relieves Henry.*)   What can it mean?

Henry [*having become insane.*]   Bloody Tiger dont kill me!—Spare my life I am inocent! —Newton did it—Georgie my child, where are you?—Sharp-Eye protect Alice!   Oh, George,—my son—catch him,—kill him,— revenge your mother! (*flash of fire from the keg; Sharp-Eye, quickly takes the keg and throws it out.*]   He is coming,—yes, he is coming;— Don't you behold him?   There,—it is Newton! [*falls to the floor.*

Sharp-Eye. [*setting fire to the building*]   The Great Spirit has revenged my father in a more fearful way than ever I contemplated. His life is now sacred; his mind however is a blank. [*takes Henry to carry him away, when at the door a flash of fire seen, and a report of a cannon is heard; the house may fall together*

42

Scene II.

A path in the forest.

Michael *appears, hands bound followed by* Ralph *revolver in hand.*

Michael. I can't proceed another step, I am so weary, that I can hardly lift my feet from the ground.

Ralph. Come, don't stop here, or I will silence you forever; you must go on!

Michael. What is that, I must? I'll show you in a minute. [*throwing himself on the ground.*

Ralph. [*aside.*] You damned Dutchman! I dare not leave him here; he must come along. (*aloud.*) Get up, you lazy scoundrel, we are not far from our destination and when we reach it you can rest yourself as much as you please.

Michael. Yes, I know, perhaps forever.

Ralph. Come, get up I say, and be quick about it.

Michael. Oh, I am in no hurry! (*Ralph stoops down to lift Michael and the latter seizes Ralph's shirt with his teeth, and throws his arms over Ralph's head and draws revolver from Ralph's pocket, which he drops to the ground. Releasing Ralph, gives him a push and recovers the revolver.*

43

and aims it at him.) Aha," the tables are turned, and now it is my turn to laugh. I am afraid that thing is too dangerous for you. Come, my boy, out with your knife, and cut these bindings! Come now, hasten lively for I am in a great hurry now! (*Ralph cuts ropes.*) Well, my traveling companion, I'm sorry but you will have to excuse me from continuing this journey in your company. Tell your captain that I'll remember his hospitality, and that Sharp-Eye and myself will soon give him a call. Go, now! or I may feed you on some of the blue beans, you have stuffed in here.

[*exit Ralph, after turning around several times.*

Michael. [*perceives Newton in distance.*] Ah, there is the captain of those bandits; I must know what he wants. [*hides himself.*

Newton. [*entering*] The old man has been blown out of existence, and I am well rid of him. His servant shall be the next, and then I'll settle with Sharp-Eye who is meddling with my business too much. When all have walked the plank, then I shall take a long rest in the lovely arms of my sweet Alice. [*exit.*

Michael. [*in the distance.*] That no good fellow is after me and the Indian! Well, mein lieber freund, I think I am after you too! [*exit.*

44

Scene III.

An Indian hut.

Henry *sleeping on a couch.* Sharp-Eye *looking at him.*

Sharp-Eye. It seems to me as if I had seen that old man's face many, many years ago. And the name of Newton, too, sounds most familiar. They come to me as if in a dream.

Henry. [*moving restlessly.*] Georgie, oh my Georgie, do not leave me again!

Sharp-Eye. The crisis is approaching. I shall soon know whether his mind will be restored.

Henry. [*sitting up.*] Minnie, my wife, dost thou hear me,–is our child Georgie, still alive? Oh, where am I? (*to Sharp-Eye.*) and who are you?

Sharp-Eye. I am your friend — Sharp-Eye, Chief of the Cherokees!

Henry. Ah yes, I have a faint remembrance. Did you not once save my life?

Sharp-Eye. Yes, I did!

Henry. Yes, yes, it is coming back to my memory, but pray tell me, where is Alice, and Michael too?

Sharp-Eye. I cannot tell; I hoped to learn that news from you.

45

Henry. From me? Oh, wait a minute till I collect my senses! let me think. (*rubbing his head.*) Now I have it. Captain Newton, the murderer of my wife, captured and carried them away.

Sharp-Eye. What is that you say? Newton, the murderer of your wife?

Henry. Yes, Newton and no one else murdered my wife, and I,— God help me for it,— I punished your father for the crime. But now I know he was innocent. Can you ever forgive me?

Sharp-Eye. You were forgiven long ago, but pray tell me who was Newton?

Henry Newton and Mortimer are one and the same person! [*sinks down on the couch, exposing a mark on his arm*

Sharp-Eye. If that is the case, I shall not stop until you are punished, Captain Newton! (*approaches the couch.*) Ah, the old man sleeps, but his mind is at ease. But what is this? Why, it is the same mark that appears on my arm! Roberson! Newton! Bloody Tiger! How familiar those names sound. Ah, I see it all now. (*looks at the floor.*) A woman murdered—and lying on the ground—her child in the arms of an Indian—a man appeared and was stabbed—while leaning over the woman—and I, —yes, yes I cried for help —no, no, it is'nt possible! can it be, that I am the son of awhite man,—can it be that he is my father? *(enter Flying Deer.)* Oh, Flying Deer, I am glad to see you, now answer me promptly and truly, am I the son of Bloody Tiger?

Flying Deer.   Can you doubt it?

Sharp-Eye. [*seizing Flying Deer by the throat*] I dont beleive it, and I think you know the truth!

Flying Deer.   I think —I—say—I will—

Sharp-Eye.   I will force you to tell the truth, now out with it; who was my father?

Flying Dear.   I—can't—tell you. [*on his knees.*]

Sharp-Eye.   You must! do you hear me? you must!

Flying-Deer.   I dare not; I have promised Bloody Tiger, never to give it away.

Sharp-Eye.   Bloody Tiger is dead.   I am your commander now and you have to confess; if you don't, I'll strangle you to death!

Flying-Deer.   No, you shall not!   Remove your hands from my throat and I'll confess the truth.

47

Sharp-Eye. Well then, be quick about it!

Flying-Deer. The blood of a pale-face runs through your veins; your father is that man there, Henry Roberson!

Sharp-Eye. Good Heaven! can it be possible?

Flying-Deer. Yes, there is your father sleeping on the couch!

Sharp-Eye. I believe you, now go, I would like to be alone. (*exit Flying-Deer.*) I will not rouse him from his sleep; he shall never learn from me that I am his son. I have lived the life of an Indian till now, and I shall continue to do so. I will seek Capt. Newton and he shall pay dearly for his cruelty to me and mine. Not one of his gang shall go out free! When I have wreaked revenge on the murderer of those who were dear to me, I may explain my identity. (*lays down to sleep. It is getting dark. Newton enters with Jim and Ralph. They seize Sharp-Eye. Michael and Flying-Deer enter, both with revolvers in their hands.*

Michael Sieh'st du wie du guckst! Yes, that's me, the Dutch Michael!

CURTAIN.

48

ACT IV.

SCENE I. *Interior view of a saloon.*

[NEWTON *and* RALPH *seated at a table.*]

Pat. [*the bartender.*] Well gents, this is my treat—my initiation in this business; from this day, I am Mrs. Mary Kraft's bartender. Here she goes!

Newton. [*appearing as an unknown.*] Well sir, I hope you will satisfy the land-lady. Is she a widow?

Pat. Be jabers she is, and a nice one too! She's as pretty as a picture, and has pluck and money.

Ralph. You want to set your cap for her!

Pat. By thunder, you are right; if I had that woman, I'd feel like a bumble bee in a pan of milk.

Mary. [*entering from the side.*] Well, Pat, how is the business?

Pat. Very good ma'am, very good!

Mary. What, you call that good, when two people is in the saloon? Go and ask them what they wish. [*Newton and Ralph take cigars.*] That was right; that's what I like. Every

49

five minutes you must go around and see if
you can't make the business go, and when
they was treat you, never say no.

Pat. No, no; I never refused to take a drink.
Why, ma'am it is the best habit I got.

Mary. Why did you not tell me so, when you
started to work here.

Pat. Oh well, you did not ask me, and I only
speak of habits, when somebody wants to
know them. [*takes a chew.*

Mary. Pat, what are you doing? don't eat that
tobacco!

Pat. No, no, I am not hungry!

Mary. By gosh, what you can lie to me. I
saw it Pat, I saw you bite off a piece!

Pat Oh, you are talking about the chew I took?

Mary. What, do you think that I don't know
what a Jew is? You couldn't swallow a Jew
with the maul you got; no sir!

Pat. Don't misunderstand me; I mean a chewing tobacco!

Mary. Chewing tobacco, you call that? Why,
man, it looked like dirt!

Pat. Yes, but it don't taste like it! [*spits on the
floor.*

Mary. But I guess, it don't taste much very

extra, then you spit as if you were paid to make a river in the hurry!

Pat. It only seems so to you, but not to the boys of this country.

Mary. Well, and what is the matter with the girls?

Pat. Oh, they know it's good too; all the girls are chewing nowadays.

Mary. Well, that is all right! The girls take Huty-pooty-doody, to keep the teeth nice and clean; then there is no man on earth who'd like to marry a woman with such black teeth as you got. Do you understand?
[*exit to the side.*

Pat. (*whistles.*) I'll bet if she would be a law-yer, she would win every case. [*Pat busies himself behind the bar.*] Say, gents, did you hear of the fire and murder in the woods, beyond?

Newton. Why no, we are strangers in these parts; tell us about it!

Pat. It is'nt much that I can tell you. They say that an Indian set fire to the house and that he and an old white man were burned to death.

Newton. This neighborhood must be in a bad smell, there are so many thieves about.

Pat. Thieves, be jabers, you are right sir! They robbed a saloon five miles from here, and nearly killed the bartender. I tell you gents, that never happens to me! I am just as good as a watch dog.

Newton. We don't doubt that, but a dog is'nt smart enough for thieves. (*to Ralph.*) Ralph, you better go back and keep an eye on Jim; I don't trust that fellow any more!

Ralph. Captain, Jim is all right! He always was on our side and he is a trustworthy comrade.

Newton. Yes, I know he is; but only as long as there is some one near him. I am certain he is very interested about our little bird and I want you to go there and see if I am right.

Ralph. All right, captain! But I think you are wrong if you take him for a treacherous fellow.

Newton. That's all right! You go and do as I told you! [*exit Ralph. Newton carefully examines a paper.*

Pat. [*admiring the bar.*] There, that looks first rate now; I think it will pass inspection. (*a tramp sneaks in and passes out several bottles and some lunch to a comrade on the outside.*) Faith, the land-lady will think the world of me, when

52

she returns, and finds every thing in its
place, and looking so bright and clean.
Sure Pat, you are a trump and might as well
have a drink with yourself!

Mary. [*entering and seeing the tramp.*] Pat, you
big fool, don't you see that tramp there,
stealing my property? Catch him, quick!
(*tramp disappears and Pat in his haste, upsets the
bar.*) Oh, holy Moses, oh my poor soul! Can
it be possible, in broad daylight too, in the
presence of myself. Oh ma'am, have pity on
poor Pat!

Mary. Get out of here, I don't want such a
green fool around me. Get a broom and dust
pan and brush up that mess on the floor!

Sharp-Eye. [*entering with Roberson,—who wears
false beard,—and seating themselves at a table.
Newton departs shaking his fist threateningly
Sharp-Eye goes to the door and looks after him.*)
Fool that you are, you think that I did not
recognize you! My name is Sharp-Eye and
an Indian bears his name only, when he is
worthy of it!

Mary. Oh, Sharp-Eye, how glad I am to meet
you again! Where did you come from? Did
you see or hear anything from my poor
Michael? I haven't heard a word from him

since he disappeared with his old master and Miss Alice. Oh, will I ever see him again!

[*weeping.*

Sharp-Eye. Be quiet ma'am, don't despair, Michael is alive and he will return to you again! (*enter Flying-Deer, who whispers softly to Sharp-Eye. The latter turns to Roberson.*) I just received good news. If I ask you to do a favor for me, will you grant it?

Henry Yes, if I can; speak out!

Sharp-Eye. Let me have the knife with which you killed Bloody Tiger!

Henry. The very same knife? yes you shall have it; here it is, take it, but do not use it in the same way which I did.

Sharp-Eye. I shall never use it against any but the guilty, and those who deserve punishment!

Newton. [*entering with the sheriff and two deputies. Newton points to Sharp-Eye.*] There is the man who killed my friend and neighbor, Roberson! Arrest him!

Sharp-Eye. You lie! I can prove it.

Newton. He speaks falsely; he is guilty of the crime, and I want you to do your duty, officer!

54

Sheriff. If he can prove his innocence, I have no authority to detain him. An Indian has as much right to the protection of the law as a white man! Now Sharp-Eye, I want you to tell me the truth. Do you know anything about Roberson's death? Who killed him?

Sharp-Eye. Nobody killed him; he is not dead but this fellow (*tearing a false beard from Newton.*) tried his best to kill him, but was foiled by me! Gentlemen, here is Mr. Roberson! [*Roberson removes a false beard.*

Newton. [*aside.*] Hades is turning against me; I must get out of here quickly. [*endeavors to escape through the door, but is caught by Michael entering.*

Michael. I've got him, I've got the rascal! [*Newton and Michael wrestle. Michael pulls off Newton's coat and falls to the floor. Newton escaping after several shots fired by Sharp-Eye.*

Mary. Oh how glad I am that my Michael has come back to me! Michael, my dear Michael, come to my arms!

Michael. Mary, my darling, I'll fly to thee!

Pat. Oh dear, oh dear, she's got him again! she's got him again!

Scene II.

A path in the woods.

Michael *appearing with* Mary.

Michael. Come on, come on, I'll show you what I will do with you.

Mary. Michael, what is the matter with you; are you verneckt? Oh, hu, don't tear me all to pieces!

Michael. Shut up, when I speak. You—you—

Mary. Well, what are you getting at. Don't be too much excited, you know well enough it won't do you any good. Do you hear?

Michael. What! I want to see about that. You know what you can do? You can live with that Irishman and I go back to Germany!

Mary. Oh, your jealousy is the reason again, that you don't know what you are doing. Well you may go; I am sure you can't go far without your dear Mary.

Michael. Yes, dear you was to me once, but now I would like to sell you very cheap, for nothing. I keep my word right away; I go back to mein old father-land, and you can marry that nice bartender, who eats tobacco.

56

Mary. Oh, Michael, good old friend, best husband of all the other husbands, stay here and do not leave me alone in this wilderness. You break my heart when you run away from me.

Michael. Oh, Mary stop, you make the stones cry with your story.

Mary. Michael; ach mein lieber Schatz, do not laugh at a loving wife. You must not go; have you forgotten that you dare not go back any more, on account of that soldier business of yours?

Michael. Yes, that's so, you are right like all ways.

Mary. Yes, and if you would listen to me every time, all the things would go a better way. What is the use to get hot-headed about Pat?

Michael. You can say so, but I,—I can't. Oh Mary, I loved you so much; all my heart was yours, but now, since I see that another man is in my house, I can't bear it any longer; I must go!

Mary. If that is all you got against him, then I tell him to quit; and if he don't, I'll discharge him.

Michael. Yes, that is right; that's the way to please your husband, mein sueser Zucker

57

klumpe. Come, I'll help you, if he don't want to move away, I will fire him out.

Mary. No, you don't, you take my advice and remain here. Your head is out of order, and you may start a fight on account of nothing. Now, I don't want you to do so. I can settle with him alone, my old Brummbaer! [*exit.*

Michael. Mein lieber Gott im Himmel she callt me an old grumbler! No, I want stand that. I know what I do if I don't shange my mind; I fire the both, out of the property of my house! (*enter Sharp-Eye.*) Say, tell me, brother, do you know anything of the place Alice has been taken to, and where she is kept; have you any idea what has become of that rascal Newton?

Sharp-Eye. I do not no where Alice is concealed, and as to that rascal Newton, I cannot imagine what has become of him.

Michael. Well, I know.

Sharp-Eye. Do you really?

Michael. Yes, have you ever been on top of Red Mountain?

Sharp-Eye. Yes, many a time; I know every nook and crook, even in the dark.

Michael. Well, I don't think you know of the place I am going to lead you to, but I will

explain it to you. You pass around Eagle
Rock, till you come to a brook; you follow up
its course, till you arrive at a huge pine tree;
when there, continue on your way for about
a hundred steps, where you will find a bridge;
on the opposite side stands a small house, in
which Alice is kept a prisoner. I tell you
this because,—well because I know that you
and Alice are sweet on each other. You
must go now, and may good luck follow you!
(*Sharp-Eye starts away.*) I shall not suffer
him to go alone; there are dangerous foes
about here, and if harm comes to Sharp-Eye,
Miss Alice would never forgive me. I have
it, I shall go and inform Roberson and the
sheriff, right straight away. [*exit, singing.*

Scene III.

*A lonely place in the mountains, showing a small hut,
in which Alice is kept a prisoner. A bridge
to be seen in the rear.*

Jim *walking to and fro.*

Alice. [*unseen.*] Jim, oh Jim!

Jim. Well girl, what is it you want?

Alice. Oh Jim, can't you let me leave this place?
If you do, my friends will give you enough
money to make you a rich man.

59

Jim. You ask for too much! I will grant you anything except your freedom.

Alice. Please Jim, open this door, and I swear that nobody shall learn that you were concerned in my escape. Jim, you had a mother once; poor old soul, she would not approve of your present course. Think of her, Jim, and let me go! [*Ralph crosses the bridge and listens.*

Jim. My dear old mother! yes indeed I am more than disgusted with the life I am leading; perhaps this is the best opportunity to turn over a new leaf and live a different and better life. Yes, I will release you, and this one good act may atone in part for some of my misdeeds, and I know you will pray for me. [*attempts to open the door, but is seized by Ralph.*

Ralph. So, my fine friend, what were you going to do?

Jim. You have been watching me, and I hope you was'nt blind!

Ralph. No, you bet! Our Captain was right when he told me to come and watch you, as he expected treachery on your part. (*they wrestle on the bridge, Jim is stabbed and thrown over the bridge.*) I am sorry for you but one life is as good as another! (*a gun is fired,*

60

Ralph drops dead and Sharp-Eye crosses the bridge, and releases Alice.

Alice. Oh Sharp-Eye, is it you? how glad I am to see you! and to think that you should be the one to give me my freedom! Oh, I thank you so much! how can I ever repay you?

Sharp-Eye. Don't speak of that now, you can best repay me by returning to your home. Your uncle is anxious to see you, and this is too dangerous a place for you.

Alice. Is it possible? Is my dear uncle alive? Oh what joyous news!

Sharp-Eye. Yes so it is! Come now, you must take this road, and here is a pistol; you may need it. Should anything serious happen to me, then ask Flying-Deer, who Sharp-Eye was. Try to think of me, if you can; as a dearly beloved brother. Be cautious and do not falter till you reach your home. Farewell!

Alice. Oh, Sharp-Eye, my dearest friend I dread to think of your remaining here alone; but, if it must be, then farewell till we meet again. [*exit Alice.*

Sharp-Eye. Somebody is coming across the bridge; at last I shall face that wretch Newton, and somebody will get hurt. [*enters the hut, removes his feathers, outer garments, etc., retaining a single knife, and then disguising himself as a girl.*

Newton. [*appearing outside of hut.*] That devil-ish Indian interfered in my affairs a second time; to him I am indebted for all my bad luck; but wait, 'he who laughs last, laughs best!' I must call the boys. Hello, there within, Jim! Ralph!—No answer? that is strange! (*peers about.*) They are both gone; —gone with the girl too! (*opens the door.*) No, that fear is groundless; the beauty is still here. (*seizes Sharp-Eye and forces him through the door.*) Here, I am going to leave this place, and if you will follow me willingly, I'll spare your life.

Sharp-Eye. [*throwing aside his mask*] Look in my face; do you recognize me?

Newton. (*amazed.*) Sharp-Eye!

Sharp-Eye. Yes, but my right name is George Roberson!

Newton. What?

Sharp-Eye. Oh, I see you still remember the little boy who made you run years ago, with a few words. That little boy is a man now, and he has sworn to kill you with the knife of Bloody Tiger! (*pulls his knife.*) Now you coward, stand up, like a man if you can, and fight for your life! (*they fight with knives, and*

62

*Roberson, Alice, Michael, Mary, Pat, the Sheriff
and deputies appear. Newton drops his knife, but
succeeds in gaining that of Sharp-Eye.*

Newton. [*to Roberson.*] By this knife your wife
fell, and now your son, shall die by the same
blade!

Roberson. Oh, I see it all now! Sharp-Eye my
son, my long lost boy!

Sharp Eye. [*to Newton.*] You told a lie! (*to
Roberson.*) Do not believe his false words!
[*Sharp-Eye throws Newton who falls on his own
knife.*]

Newton. Oh,—oh,—I am dying!

Alice. Oh, look here, Sharp-Eye is wounded!

Roberson. [*examining Sharp-Eye's wound and perceiving the birth-mark on his arm.*] Newton
spoke the truth indeed! you are my long lost
son George; this mark proves it!

Sharp-Eye. Father, it is true! I knew it long
ago, but I could not tell you of it on account
of Newton. [*they embrace.*

Roberson. There, my son, now go to Alice; she
is worthy of you, and may God bless you both!

Mary. [*to Michael.*] Why, Michael, what is the
matter with you? I do believe you are cry-
ing. [*they embrace.*

63

Michael. Yes, yes, too much happiness at once!

Pat. Oh, murder, so much affection overcomes me! (*turning around, Newton gets up and staggers to the bridge.*) Holy Moses, the rascal is still alive! Sheriff, sheriff, seize him! [*Flying-Deer blocks Newton's escape. Newton hangs in mid-air, from the bridge.*

Newton. Mercy, have mercy on me!

Michael. Not to you; you do not deserve any mercy!

Flying-Deer, Hoi, hoi, hoi, ugh, ugh! Flying-Deer will send the pale-face to the happy hunting ground. [*forces Newton to release his hold.*

Roberson. A miserable end it was, but he richly deserved it. Society has been well rid of one of the worst of human monsters. Oh, God we thank thee for our deliverance from the many perils which have beset us.

[THE END.]